The Moving Finger writes; and, having writ,
Moves on: nor all thy Piety nor Wit
Shall lure it back to cancel half a Line,
Nor all thy Tears wash out a Word of it.

~ Omar Khayyám, Rubáiyát,
trans. Edward FitzGerald

Other Books by Bob MacKenzie

Poetry

Agapé: Heaven & Earth, Dark Matter Press, 2015
Spirit Quest (with Sharlena Wood, artist), Dark Matter Press, 2014
On Edge, Dark Matter Press, 2012
Songrise, Dark Matter Press, 2012
Innocent (I wasn't there), Thee Hellbox Press, 2008
Audio-Visuals, Sarnia Public Art Gallery, 1973
Reflection, self-published, 1966

Prose Fiction

The Hired Gun (Mike St. Pierre, illustrator), Dark Matter Press, 2016
Another Eternity, Dark Matter Press, 2012
A Gathering of Shadows, Dark Matter Press, 2012
Ghost Shadow: Unfinished Sins, Dark Matter Press, 2010
To Whom It May Concern, Dark Matter Press, 2010
A Beautiful Day to Be Dead (collaboration), Thee Hellbox Press, 2008
To Whom It May Concern (e-book), Amazon Shorts, 2006
Ghost Shadow: Unfinished Sins (hypertext), Poet Pourri, 1999
The Little Song, Brandstead Press, 1975

somewhere still in wind
the tree is bending

Bob MacKenzie

Silver Bow Publishing
720 Sixth Street, Unit # 5
New Westminster, BC
CANADA V3L 3C5

Title: somewhere still in wind the tree is bending
Author: Bob MacKenzie
Cover Art: 'Survival' by Richard Gold
Layout & Design: Candice James
© 2018 Silver Bow Publishing

Library and Archives Canada Cataloguing in Publication MacKenzie, Bob, 1947-, author Somewhere still in wind the tree is bending / Bob MacKenzie. Includes index. Poems. Issued in print and electronic formats. ISBN 978-1-927616-75-8 (softcover).–ISBN 978-1-927616-76-5 (PDF) I. Title. PS8575.K424S66 2018 C811'.54 C2018-903257-X C2018-903258-8

Foreword

In cooking, often a recipe needs only to be introduced to an onion to
achieve the perfect flavour. The flavour of this collection would not be
all that it is without the support and patience of a very special onion
who has become an important part of the stew that is my life.

I also thank poets John Ambury, Joseph Anthony Farina, and Meg Freer
who have looked over the manuscript for this book and offered
valuable suggestions; the many individuals in all the poetry
communities through which I have passed and who have given helpful
suggestions on various of these poems; and family and friends who
have been so supportive of me over the course of my career.

Acknowledgements

Versions of some of the poems in this collection have been previously
published by: Alien Pub Magazine, Alive, Big Pond Rumours, Free Lit
Magazine, Generation, Literary Review of Canada, Modicum, Ottawa
Poetry Magazine, Quoin, Rat's Ass Review, Speak Out, Special Song,
Stanza Room Only, Stimulus, Thee Hellbox Press, The Tower, and
Ultraviolet Magazine. The long poem "Edge" is indebted to many
sources and influences, including: Desiderata (Max Ehrmann), Howl
(Allen Ginsberg), If I Had a Hammer (Pete Seeger & Lee Hays), Still Falls
the Rain (Dame Edith Sitwell), The Hollow Men (Thomas Stearns Eliot),
The Love Song of J. Alfred Prufrock (Thomas Stearns Eliot), The
Rubáiyát of Omar Khayyám (trans. Edward Fitzgerald), The Second
Coming (William Butler Yeats) The Sound of Silence (Paul Simon & Art
Garfunkel), The Spirit of Radio (Geddy Lee Weinrib, Alex Lifeson, and
Neil Peart), and What Have They Done to the Rain? (Malvina Reynolds

Table of Contents

scene

you start out with just one thing:
a person, place, or object.

for example:

this woman in the large hat,
skirts blowing around her legs.

you look around her closely,
learn where she is standing now:

see her close by the lamp post
in the cone of light at dusk.

standing forlorn in the rain,
is she there to meet someone?

who has drawn this woman here,
could it be her secret love?

ask yourself what happens next
in the rain on the corner.

for example:

a black sedan approaches,
stops and the rear door opens.

had you noticed the music
blended with the sound of rain?

softly heard in the background,
music sets the scene's blue mood.

there's a threat now, a tension
music's attack escalates.

the black sedan vanishes
along the dark rainy street.

there is only the lamplight;
there is only the soft rain.

cut and print.

meeting

there are poems
outside
what I write

poets beside me
burning bushes
they made themselves

why choose one
smile for the cat's
jive is more hep

blowing crazy lines
Cheshire and glib
ivories glinting dark

between webbed branches
crimson lip
synchs that flick open

mouthed words like cats
have teeth and they
glisten pearly white

in the shower
bloody makeup runs
singing in the rain

not words but scat
the safe refrain
from unknown forms

words don't do
do they at times like
this outside time

you face lips suspended
bleeding in the rain
burning in the bush

the words are not the same

the words are not the same,
and yet, they are somehow
the same words we have
used so many times

before we found our way
of using words alone
as meanings slipped
away from us, we talked

the words together meaning
what we together decided
and yet, they were somehow
not what we meant at all

to say in that brief space
and time in those few words
all there was we had
to say was not the same

message after message passed
between us in silent codes
after the words had passed
beyond our comprehension

of the words and meanings
we created ourselves, the words
alone and meanings separate,
we too grew apart in silence

read aloud

the words don't matter
here only
caress wash ravage rush
through and across
senses of sound
writ everywhere

it is not written
it is not
                written
it is
         not written

the moving finger
writes but having
writ leaves
cold stone remains

take two
and call me
he said
         not wrote
call me
         not write

right
the power is
not in but
behind and before
the words

in the beginning
perhaps
but thought
sound and light
energy pure
and simple

electric power
also
were and were
with
the first and all
saying by
          eye gesture intonation
          flow flux howl rant rave
dance fire smoke captive
          words undone
doing

here the power is
only
          the words
don't matter

A Thought Rides the Wind

A thought rides
and soaring above,
like a feathery autumn leaf
or a hawk at the hunt.
A thought drifts,
ever upward, ever upward.
A thought rides the wind.

Time and the Prophet

Borne on the storm,
father before
followed the ledge –
thunder his foe,
lightning his load,
upward the peaks.
Ever the wind,
searching for peace
over the clouds.

Born of the storm,
I am the door hung on the edge –
you are my foe,
(what is my load?)
climbing the peaks.
Ever the wind,
promising peace
over the clouds.

she says

she feels like metaphors
with diamond sharp edges

words flung on the table
in the space between us
not meant to puzzle me
but inform me of what

she can't say otherwise

Elsa

There is a rustle in your name, like the
passing of the years; the sound of days
falling like leaves around you, inevitably
to leave a barren scarecrow in the wind
without a rustle.

There is already a look of scarecrow in
your eyes, a certain hollow in your face
and hunger in your mien that can only grow,
like Chaos, inward upon itself.

There is a beauty about you, but it is the
derelict fantasy of a long vacant mansion
or the prairie in November rather than
that of youth in search of life.

There is a rustle that follows you as you
move, carrying autumn from room to room
and filling every room with leaves until,
one day, you shall have shed so much of
yourself that none shall be left for the present.

Friction Drive

Man must lose himself in action
Lest he wither in despair

T. W. Pylypiuk, July '71

What cash cropping self can say
which is the harvest?
Unrelenting action or
perhaps Action's end?
I cannot say which profits,
unending planting,
harvesting and planting, or
anticipating
the seasons as they pass
and no effort spent.
I only know if I stop –
then I shall stop dead

reflections in a gallery

black and white photo of a homeless child
abandoned to the dangers of the streets,
peering from a dark space between buildings,
the dusk-light stippled like an engraving.

hand on his top hat a man scurries past,
looks away as bitter wind grabs at the child,
fails to see this child pull worn rags tighter,
believes everything is alright and walks on.

one hundred years later razed neighbourhoods
give rise to gentrified condos and lofts and
unseen in the shadows the tattered children
bring unreasoning fear of the downtrodden.

Hard Times Come Again

Seeing old news photos of men
in long Depression bread lines
my mother noticed mostly this:
no matter how hard times were
 the men's shoes were polished,
creased pants freshly pressed
and their hair neatly combed.

As a kid in mid-century prairie
towns broken by the recession
I saw men, old I thought, sitting
on benches, porches or chairs
by buildings grey as they were
with work clothes freshly washed,
shoes polished and hair combed.

Youth unable to find employment
now sit on sidewalks downtown
or outside stores in strip malls
sometimes wrapped in blankets,
paper coffee cup set in front,
thrift shop clothes laundered,
worn boots clean and hair combed.

boundaries

this is what you don't know
we're all very afraid

this is what you do know
we're all very afraid

we block out the terrors
but lock the fear inside

this is what I do know

there are walls here
they are your walls

the least of these

    I

nineteenth century
painting of poverty
she stands in rags
framed against
the black of late
december midnight
in my doorway

her three knocks
brought me
not quite awake
to the door
and now
this apparition
hunches before
my hazy eyes
unreal

a cracked voice
can I use your phone
like a dream
a nightmare
she scares me

I don't have
a phone
I lie

again
the voice
my feet are
freezing
and I am
unsure why
I am afraid

I close the door

when I open
the door again
she is gone
spirit in the dark
lost in the mist
like she was
never there

II

near dark river
waters the marsh
late december
desolate
lost in thought
I stand by
a park bench
in the grey
half light

something
knocks my ankle
sudden and hard
startles me
from my frozen
reverie
like a door
opening

at my feet
a muskrat drags
himself broken
toward the water

plaintive eyes
a quiet voice
asking me to do
something

his feet frozen
as he stalls
and dies

The Flower

The bell tolled low:
scarcely heard at first.

An itinerant artist saw her once
when he came painting five dollar
faces of pedestrians.

He saw her and was intrigued
by thoughts that filled
her eyes
and worlds she held
in her skilled hands
and strong will.

Sitting,
her back to the wall
as a defence against
the electric wind
sparking around her
and chilling.

He saw her
and offered
free
to paint her
portrait.

The Flower Lady portrait was painted.

There is in a business window
where she walked
a haunting portrait
of the Flower Lady.

She sits
back to the wall
face to the wind's short circuits

city grey
gazing into distance
at green European fields
or a warm farm home
where a young girl
once lived.

She sits
back to the wall
face to the wind
a basket of flowers
at her feet.

The bell tolled.

She was
the Flower Lady
she needed
no more identification
than that.

She rose with alley cats
and young babies
she rose with the crisp
morning sun and sea breeze
and was sometimes
in her place at market's head
as early as seven
in the morning.

She took
brightly coloured materials
in the beginning
and created
flowers she sold
all over the city.

There was a restaurant
where she ate
(if you can call it that)

a bit of tea and a bit of toast,
not much of either.

She sat alone
caring for her creations,
her nearly flowers,
pinching and shaping limp petals
straightening green green leaves.

Then she ate
her usual late
evening lunch:
tea and toast.
That was all.

The bell tolled.

It was often midnight
before she returned
to her room
with her left over not quite
flowers.

If the sun hung
like a halo
the glow of its ring
burning her eyes
and dropping burning summertime
to her shoulders,
she walked.

If the sea threw its net
of fog over her,
no matter:
she walked.
If winter
wrapped cold claws
around her
and dug icy teeth
into her,
she walked.

One man recalls
one cold and foggy night
she knocked
on his door at eleven at night
a good part
of her bouquets
unsold.

She lived
chiefly
on tea and toast.

She hoarded her small cash reserve
for materials
to create
nearly, not quite flowers.

For twenty-two years
she occupied the same room
had no guests
or visitors
who were seen.

No relative came
to call
on the Flower Lady.
The bell tolled.

She was
herself like a flower:
a thin wildflower
bright and alive
like the mayflowers
she sold in the spring.

Sometimes she wore
a fresh, crisp bandana.
Sometimes
her grape basket
was gaily decorated

like a happy moment
in childhood.
Sometimes it was plain.

The tributes are many

    she was always neat and tidy;
    she would not take charity;
    once when her kindly landlady
    turned down a three dollar payment
    she wanted to make on her rent,
    she went out and bought her a gift
    in the same amount.

Everything reported
serves to enhance her
memory.

When her death
was announced
few noticed.

The bell tolled low:
She needed
no more identification
than that.

leaving it behind

she walks with the wind at her back
as though escaping something dark
she knows cannot be far behind

she stops and her shoulders shudder
forcing tears she holds back to come
then she walks on more quickly now

she feels the shadow at her back
following always following
has known this dark force far too long

in summer's bright noonday sunshine
she walks in the dark and shivers
not from cold but some old terror

nobody sees the fear in her eyes
few even notice she is there
a woman walking through shadows

this dark she knows is inside her
buried for years but now haunting
all her sleeping or waking dreams

nobody knows why she ends it
they only see a pretty girl
not the fear she has left behind

The Girl

The voices are there hidden in the night
where the girl can hear their every word
hidden behind corners and whispering
secrets along the street and in the trees

She shivers in the darkness and moves on
knowing the shadows follow and whisper
not only secrets but darker threats
all in languages only she understands

Somewhere near an owl's hollow hoot calls her
her name echoes off the city's hard walls
cats' wails follow in a bitter harmony
the girl only half understands but fears

The street falls silent but the girl hears still
shadows whispering darkly toward her
the hush following her every step
she falling into ever deeper dark

Sometimes the girl hears footsteps behind her
she turns to look but sees only the darkness
she sees the shadows slide along the walls
 she shivers in the darkness and moves on

There is no sky behind the ink of night
the moon hides behind a black mask of clouds
someone has broken the streetlight bulbs
the voices are there hidden in the night

She shivers in the darkness and moves on
shadows move slowly along the dark walls
shadows whisper dark threats only she hears
she shivers and moves on through the darkness

Somewhere far away a siren shrieks out
the siren bounces lightly off the walls
The girl hears only voices that follow
she hears only the whispers in the dark

A far away siren meets the darkness
the wail underscores a doo-wop song
owl and cat harmonize with the siren
the girl hears but only half understands

The girl is alone in the darkest night
a darkest night hides deep inside the girl
there is no escape from the voices' whispers
there is no escape from the creeping dark

Somewhere near an owl's hollow hoot calls her
an owl in the city how strange she thinks
her name bounces off hard walls into black
cat's wails follow her name into the dark

The girl hears voices no other can hear
she hears and she understands dark whispers
threats in the night touch the girl deep within
hide behind corners and whisper to her

The dark grows thicker to smother the girl
not ink now the dark becomes living tar
the girl is wrapped in a black tar blanket
from somewhere the girl hears a siren call

The voices are there hidden in the night
she shivers in the darkness and moves on
somewhere near she hears an owl's hollow call
the street falls silent but the girl hears still

Sometimes the girl hears footsteps behind her
she shivers in the darkness and moves on
there is no sky behind the ink of night
somewhere far away a siren calls her

Night's dark blanket scares her only a while
deep in her heart she feels new warmth growing
she drowns in night's warm comforting embrace
falling into deep sleep the siren wakes her

Fear releases the girl and blankets the warmth
in her heart is only the darkness she fears
in the night there is nobody to save her
there is only the shadows and the song

a scream slices the dark startling the girl
a scream seems to come from her own body
nobody hears nobody hears but her
she turns toward the darkness and moves on

Somewhere in the night a doo-wop song plays
dark harmonies draw her into darkness
the dark rhythm carries past some threshold
carries the girl toward dark beyond night

The voices are there hidden in the night
where the girl can hear their every word
and shivers in the darkness and moves on
and knows the shadows follow and whisper

Shadows whisper from deep in dark corners
secrets told on the street and in the trees
not only secrets but darker threats
told in languages only she understands

The girl is alone in the dark crying
nobody hears nobody knows but her
the girl follows a sound through the darkness
from somewhere she hears a doo-wop melody

Dark voices whisper to her through the night
threats in the night touch the girl deep within
somewhere far away a siren shrieks out
somewhere near she feels something dark approach

She sees only shadows hears only the song
nobody hears nobody knows but her
She shivers in the darkness and moves on
shadows follow slowly along dark walls

The girl hears voices no other can hear
she hears and she understands dark whispers
there is no escape from the whispered voices
there is no escape from the creeping dark

The doo-wop music draws the girl deeper
dark harmonies pull her toward darkness
the girl walks deeper into the darkness
there is no escape from the creeping dark

The voices are there hidden in the night
the girl hears but cannot escape them
hidden behind corners and whispering
secrets through the trees and along the street

The scream echoes louder in the darkness
there is no escape from the creeping dark
there is no escape from screams in the night
the girl has lost her way in the darkness

Shadows move slowly along the dark walls
She shivers in the darkness and moves on
knows the shadows follow her and whisper
whisper dark threats that only she can hear

Something in the night reaches deep in her
she shivers and walks into the darkness
she drowns in night's warm comforting embrace
the girl falls into perfect sleep to dream

The sun shines brightly from clear blue skies
threatening voices and dark shadows hide
the girl is at peace in a perfect day
far away a doo-wop song fills the air

the woman

it begins with a room
pale red and cool blue light
scattered silhouettes at tables
soft saxotones wafting
through cigarette smoke
and casual conversation

at the bar a splash of light
seems meant to expose
the woman who waits
slowly sips her drink
waits for something
waits for someone
waits deep in a shadow
no light can erase

sorrow bends the woman
leans her forward
slumped with elbows
abject on the bar
slow sipping her drink

on the woman's right cheek
a tear draws a damp line
downward echoed by sax
lines cutting the smoke
underlining her blue mood
another tear slides
another tear and another

the woman knows nothing
will happen now at this bar
the woman knows nobody
will come to meet her here
the woman knows nobody
knows her sorrow
what she has lost

 the music stops

the woman stands
a quick perhaps furtive
glance at near human
silhouettes in the smoke
walks slowly to the door l
lets in the sunshine
only for a moment

there is only the sax
again caressing the air
and the sad silhouettes
under red and blue lights

the woman is gone

jazz café

blowing sax
in dank basement
beatnik café
shadows stippled
begets
daguerreotype
images

cleo laine
sings bombastic
bunk
as john
dankworth blows
copacetic jazz riffs
into the night

an unroofed
suburban
foundling
in the corner
whispers
absquatulated
softly

the word lost
in reefer
smoke
poets read
cleo sings soft
dankworth wails
jazz soothes

photograph

the woman stands
frozen in time

her mirrored self
stands worlds away

each statuesque
watches herself

from further back
the shutter clicks

photographer snaps
from the mirror

in the shadows
an empty gown

upstairs the dogs howl

the anger wails breathless words at her
fast as slam poetry or dark rap
beat-boxing and pounding her soul

her anger echoes through the black riff
resounding across the space between
widening cracks where once had been love

this raw call and response will not end
echoes across the void between them
 while the dogs howl a dark harmony

Darlene

1954
lives next door
in poverty

two room
lady
lost in time
screams
          through walls
          through time

you
you did this
               to me

you
did   won't
do this again
to me

she
          her voice
recedes
          another room
          another time
distant other
voice

Gene Autry
Christmas songs
Hank Snow
          Thompson
          Williams
Carl Smith
          Perkins
Patsy Cline
               I'm Movin' On

                    Move It On Over
                    Walkin' After
Midnight

she never
sleeps
roams these two
rooms
            out of time
            out of space
sound
of her and music
from fifty-four
her world

you
did this
to me

and I will dance

in her place upstairs her music is playing
her music is playing with a solid beat
like her heart reaching out in mid-afternoon
not loud but felt in the apartment below

her music is playing with a solid beat
her pumping heart only just heard through the floor
through the ceiling of the apartment below
where another sits and finds fault with the world

her music is playing with a solid beat
her heartbeat spreading softly out the window
her heartbeat fading across the neighbours' lawns
to pause where the children play in the sunshine

from the place downstairs anger cries out loudly
against the beat against the beat of her heart
against the world in unfair rage against her
unfair and angry and she will take no more

her heart is pumping the words she cries out loud
I will bring over the neighbourhood children
I will bring over all the neighbour children
and I will dance
                 and I will dance
                            and I will

Ants

Ants on a serpent's egg,
we may crack the shell
with our bolts of Thor–
and where shall we be then?

When this serpent hatches,
being afflicted,
will he then doglike
engulp tormentor tail?

Will this Midgardian
swallow all, abyss
before recycling–
ultimate cannibal?

Heartburn

I,
Ulcer Earth
Shall devour the Universe
Duodenum outward
Spreading
Fever-Man,
Acid-Man
Devouring
Burning Sky
High thoughts
Centering on Eternity
With a stomach ache

Pyramid – a trilogy

I (Generation)

We are all building pyramids of sticks:
Pyramids we live in,
Pyramids we worship,
Pyramids we cook on,
Pyramids we die for;
Pyramids of sticks aiming to the sky.

Our commerce now turns a spinning wheel pace
Like a world of its own
Ever rolling, rolling
With bigger sticks to pile:
Temple, home, and fortress
Buttress pointing, ever pointing skyward.

The farms have grown now and the towns have too
As we draw our lines on this drifting ball –
And build an atlas all our own, with fence,
Demarcating wood showing who lives where,
Each man planting, weeding, harvesting crops
Without ever fouling another's way.

Church becomes ritual, unfeeling play –
Man is creator creating dragons;
Dragons to build cities – a work free world.
Farmers will farm or they'll move to the towns
And the town people look to the cities.
How the cities grow. Oh, how they do grow!

Machines eat man as men ate rabbits once;
A bit at a time, slowly consuming
First the mind then all his body slowly
Until machine man and machine are one:
Automatons building automatons
Destroying men endlessly. Endlessly!

The Nation is all and second is Church
And nothing matters more
Until we win this war;
Our god will defend us
And our weapons will too –
Triumph to Church and glory to Nation!

War seems to grow on men like parasites,
Single, double, triple,
Eroding human rights
Hardly with a ripple
In collective conscience
'Til, war past, we become subservient.

II (Degeneration)

We fight – wars come, wars go – growing, growing
Until two wars worldwide have come and gone.
We join the church in crying peace on Earth
And our young men defend their land of birth.
Youngsters rotting baring dried bone
Fought and died for lack of understanding.

A voice in howl cries out for all beatitude:
Tiger lily growing skyward paints a red gash
Like sunset red and fluffy white clouds overhead.
Mushroom sporing white on blue skies, a fearful badge;
A cry, a sign to all that all may soon be dead.
Warning skull and crossbones that turns the Earth to ash;
The wasteland comes to prove our most rash aptitude.

We have fought the war to end all war, twice,
Skybirds through blue, childlike hands reach outward,
Hands across a world of many secrets.
What fool is this who calls this child coward
Who, eternity lost, has no regrets.
Groping, searching, we are lurching forward.
Eden's children lost, ourselves we ask, "Thrice?"

We play with deadly aim a game, revolution,

Our board-blocks of anarchy and oldness.
Godless pawns are people bent by winds prevailing,
Strange new battle lines in evolution.
All around as people leave each church is falling
And we spawn a cloud of dark and coldness;
Even sages have no time to find solution.

Under mushroom skies, field and street, masses meet, butt
Bent on proving points to turn opinion.
Comes a cry from out the mass, "Your god is dead-dead."
Crossing minds with potions masses bleat, but
Comes a cry to all who hear, "What god then is there?"
Lost indeed to most seems God's dominion,
"He must be dead." Drugged, they slam his door with feet, shut.

War and revolution now are rampant lifestyles:
See, the desolation and ruins for miles and miles-
Misty miles of smoke, what better battle grounds, eh?
Out there somewhere grows a tree that few men seek now.
In the minds of men a lily grows, a red gash
Haling all to sinister thought like a dread lash,
Each to think a thought that each knows not how to say.

"Who is friend" each cries yet each will find no answer;
Black clouds grow where grew the tree; man's born to battle
Birdwing gone and blue too; who can name this dancer,
Only he can tell in truth the dancing's ending.
Dance on how long dance on, each display your mettle,
Somewhere still in wind the tree is bending.

III (Regeneration)

Silence-
Earth, the Earth, stands still waiting
While light climbs the horizon,
A steeplejack of the sky
Above the trace of pyramids, Stick piles aiming to the sky.

Birds sing,
A few at first but singing

And growing to a concert;
Plants sing in bright counterpoint
Their melody of colour–
Steeplejack has topped his pole.

Lovely now the day, the sun,
The creatures gathering 'round;
Here a deer, a grouse, a dog;
There a hare, a porcupine,
All enjoying spring at last
In the greening summer sun.

Here and there the pyramids
Break and fall in piles from age–
Stick piles pointing to the sun;
Higher, ever higher piles
Points to the sun in glory
Crumbling.

Animals and plants alike
Feel spring, feel life, feel all's right:
A unity fills the wind
In this abundant garden
Where all enjoy their springtime
Commune.

Abundance is life for all,
And all enjoy abundance.
Sol climbs up and down his pole
As green, brown, and white rotate
Soft streams of sand and sifting time–
Piling life-grain pyramids.
In the clearing a shadow;

He in the shadow gazes
Downward to a pile of sticks:

Pyramiding in his mind,
Pyramiding fallen sticks,
Pyramiding...

Long Time Passing

In Asia, the cherry flowers bloom
with beauty and with light.

There are legends:
of Asian dragons, of English dragons;
of a knight, George,
who saved a princess by slaying a dragon;
of a boy, George,
who confessed to slaying his father's cherry tree;
of a dark nation who believed itself the light of the world;
of a long ago, faraway war that dark nation started and lost, but never
 confessed was a wrongful invasion or a war;
of a mystic cycle of war and destruction,
of light against dark;
of a man, George,
who started a faraway war,
who thought he was saving the world
but only opened its sores; of another man, George,
who started a faraway war,
who said he was saving the world but only wanted revenge.

The words of this poem were written during that long ago, faraway war
 but apply as much now as then.

The dragon is a cherry tree;
The damsel in its knotted arms
Protected by the silver knight,
The cherry dies by battle axe.

And there they saint this chopper George;
But where he slept the cherry grows
And when he died, a cherry cross,
A cherry cross he carried then.

His mast was square when he was young;
But fire has burned his crossbrace thin
And bent the ends to arrogance,
And where have all the cherries gone?

mark: my words

this is the song of sorrow
this is the time for change
this is the time of darkness
this is the song of light

the snakes are in the water
the fires burn on the hills
and what's become of Mary
as smoke comes rolling down

wars rage in the eastern world
there's rumours more will come
all these things must come to pass
but yet it's not the end

dark washes across the land
sorrow shadows every heart
hope has gone from many hearts
the void brings black despair

famine spreads across the lands
pestilence thrives and grows
the earth herself quakes in fear
thus begins all sorrows

we become our own disease
beware air and water
beware food designed to kill
the shades are taking form

where some become offended
some betray their friends
one fears and hates the other
prophets raise smoke and mirrors

prophets say this is the end
black smoke comes rolling down

what's to become of Mary
as fires burn all around

there are serpents in the streets
snakes are in the water
rumours of wars beget wars
darkness begets monsters

the sun and moon are darkened
the stars fall from the sky
when we see the light again
light's fire will bring the end

wait until the end they say
all seems desolate now
light waits somewhere in the dark
death waits in the shadows

old men murder youth in war
philosophy preaches death
wizards poison food and drink
oh Mary don't you weep

the snakes are in the water
the fires burn on the hills
and what's become of Mary
as smoke comes rolling down

this is the song of sorrow
this is the time for change
somewhere a candle still burns
somewhere the light still shines

there is a new renaissance
there is protest and hope
the future is ours to build
this is the end my friend

cocktails in a well-lit room

all the darkness,
packaged in ceramic shells
by unknown hands so long ago
as Midgard to some certain future,
hides in Trojan eggs,
rides on mannequins,
waits to broach some foreseen gates
but goes unseen
as brilliance rises from the pit
and poltergeist,
unknown by me,
you take from my table;
you toss what you take;
you take from my table;
you toss what you take;
you hope the egg will break –
all the darkness
prematurely spilling,
hatching, not some Dark Phoenix
but a cuddly yellow chick –
all the darkness
packaged in ceramic shells
remains: not flooding,
filling the pit with ink
or whatever, although
some cracks do appear
and somewhere, not too far,
I hear the creaking,
ancient gates begin to open.

black rain

though there's no way to confirm
they say this storm began
on the other side of the world
perhaps in Fukushima or Israel
spread rapidly
wrapping everything
everywhere in darkness

a squirrel has died
above the ceiling tiles
in the hallway
outside my office

there are hundreds
everywhere
huge black flies

for so long
the storm has not abated
I've lost track of the days
spent under these
black clouds of ash
and the heavy rain
they bring with them

the streets
have become rivers
only the most courageous
and the foolish
venture out

from the window
in my office
I see the bodies
in the streets
whenever the fire
rains from the sky

some say it's a sign from some god
predicted by ancient prophets
punishment for all the evils
of mankind
others say it's our own fault
abusing the natural order
with our science

it all sounds the same to me

all I know is
for more days than I can calculate
I've not left this campus
crawling like a rat
through the tunnels
to other buildings
then back to my office
with what food and supplies
I can scrounge

there are others too
students and professors
and university staff
wandering the tunnels

I do my best to avoid them
in their eyes
there's a desperation
I believe will become
dangerous

best to play it safe

refugee blues

you have to grant relief

it took a long time before we asked
till we got used to sleeping on the floor

you can get used to almost anything

mostly it's quiet
people are just tired and quiet
and you go back home.

or you go and sit with hundreds of others
or you just up and leave

here it's like that too
you feel it in the air
you see it in the eyes

I don't much care
I just want it to end

today it was sunny at last
the clouds yesterday were black
and then today sun

who will rise up against evil
who stand up against iniquity

there was still the wind
and the cold sun shining

the breeze got too brisk
so I nodded goodbye
made my way to the moors

brought back a jar of water

Scarred

I have held the rim's curve,
fingertipping,
and have hung so, wheelbound,
fasterclipping, peered beyond my fingers,
spied the scarmarks
on the other side's face,
painted starsparks
and moons of blue and dead.

Come now, come late,
I have held this rim's curve –
this paper plate.

The New Police

You start a war nobody wants or thinks is just,
then you send young men and women overseas to fight that war; you
indoctrinate them to believe everyone is the enemy
and even apparent civilians are just enemies in disguise,
then you put them in the field for five years or more
killing civilian adults and children because they may be enemies.

After a while these young men and women come home;
you give them jobs in local and state law enforcement;
you rationalize that they have the training after all,
then you give them military weapons and vehicles
just like the ones they used in war to kill civilians.

What did you think would happen?

traveller

at his funeral, standing near his grave
a band plays The Internationale slow
and the few who stand there at his graveside
sing out still familiar words of hope

he would not have wanted some hypocrite
preaching life everlasting over him
so an old communist speaks of past times
and of fallen near-forgotten comrades

Lenin and Trotsky stand at his graveside
chilling the hearts they had once filled with hope
Uncle Joe is banned for being rowdy
and Marx's words provide the eulogy

recalling Joe Hill and legends of Wobblies
some sing Solidarity Forever;
recalling long ago ideals and passions
others wonder what their lost cause had won

grey men stand around a hole in the earth
tossing in handfuls of forgotten dreams,
manifestos, and songs, then silence comes
somewhere near the edge an old woman weeps

all the old men

all the old men walk like Walter Brennan
carry their canes like swords for self-defence
hunch 'round tables in and outside cafes
discuss times past without love or regret
circle tables to keep out modern times

Leaving America

I

Moving was never easy
not across town
not to a new city
a faraway state.

This was America
a new job for dad
good schools
new friends
mom said.

That was our life
growing up
in Fifties America.

My world was never
Father Knows Best
American Graffiti
perfect.

II

My world died
Kennedy was killed
King was killed
Bobby was killed.

There was the war
away in the eastern world
not my war
not mine.

Old enough to kill
I felt the draft
blowing my way.
Something had died

deep in my homeland
deep in my heart
that would never live
after this.

III

I could have stayed
could have signed up
I suppose fought
as some did and died
perhaps.

I was afraid
not of joining
not of fighting
but of America
what it had become.

IV

Moving was not easy
not out of America
not to a strange city
to another land
so different yet
so much the same.

Not just an immigrant
I was a refugee
a stranger
in a strange land.

Draft-dodger to some
coward and traitor
even in Canada.

Some called me and others
political freedom fighters
conscientious objectors.

Americans in Canada
unable to ever go home
we only felt very alone.

V

An amnesty was announced.
Most of us in Canada
didn't trust this amnesty
didn't trust America
anymore.

Fearing a trap
most of us stayed
put on ill-fitting
Canadian identities
became uneasy citizens
in our new land.

VI

Half a century later
estranged from our home
many of us have died
not from war but old age
and regret.

This betrayal
of us and by us
remains a cancer
in our hearts.

VII

I have no regret
that I left America
only that America
made leaving necessary
took from me
my home.

I cannot forget.

mosaic

a mosaic is only an arrangement
a convenient image made of tiles
laid upon sands which may shift
with the weight of time passing

out of ancient sands voices cry
from between the mosaic tiles
bringing up the ancient earth
and the peoples of Turtle Island

something in the dig has broken
cracked the fair vision's surface
revealing darker sands underneath
where ancient cultures are waiting

a mosaic is only an arrangement
a transitory image that can change
as the earth moves beneath the tiles
and ancient voices can be heard

as cracks appear among the tiles
voices from the distant past call
to be heard and to be reconciled
not buried in some dusty corridor

deep in an archaeological museum
people weep for the stolen children
people weep for the murdered women
people weep and the mosaic cracks

how the light gets in

back in the corner among death and brown blight
the first wild rose has appeared in my garden
a miracle of resurrection promising renewed life

heavy mist shrouds my garden in the early morning
not so much soft-focus as ominous and foreboding
a portent of dark beginning to befall the world

still somewhere distant and fading I hear birdsong
a voice of hope that briefly cuts through this mist
slightly softens the chill in the air and in my bones

in this early morning light what's not brown is grey
a sunless black and white world waiting death to come
yet here's a rose and there a bird singing and I wait

I wait watching for more omens to appear good or bad
and the poet has told us there's a crack in everything
so I watch for the crack to open up and for the light

through eternity I stand at this window and I watch
see the wild rose rise through the dead weeds and mist
hear the songbird's voice fade quaver start to return

out of the concrete sky I hear geese as they pass by
less honking than barking like a pack of dogs hunting
and I wonder just what it is they pursue so fervently

the sound of geese draws my attention up to the clouds
clouds like a grey wall of concrete barring all light
and I watch and I wait perhaps to see those four horses

ever so slight a crack is appearing in the concrete sky
light forcing the crack wide and bleeding into the mist
painting the grey of my garden shades of green and gold

there's hope here and for now I breathe a relieved sigh
begin to see the importance of this crack in everything
begin to know in my heart that's how the light gets in

edge

I've been standing in the cold falling rain
hearing the pulse of its heart beat down
seeing the dark images in its shadows
like the visions of ancient prophets
and I have seen that I stand in the gutter
between the edges between worlds apart
between gay and straight between rich and poor
between capital and commune between woman and man
between every possible polarity you can dream
looking at those edges not from the other side
but from somewhere between which is nowhere
and I have disappeared

don't get me wrong and don't get it twisted
it may after all have been only a dream
it may be I have seen nothing at all
and there was nothing at all to see in the rain
nothing but a magic shadow-show played in a box
lit by sun and moon against silhouettes of rain
around which we phantom figures come and go
the rain falling like knives slicing the dark
to create worlds then wash them away in a flash
lit by lightning that wakes me with a start

the words of the prophets echo down the centuries
truth grown tired and worn until the words are only dust
choking off the little breath we gasp to survive
the uncertain future we have created for ourselves
and in the words we hear echoing somewhere distant
the pulsing of a heartbeat pounding like a hammer
and feel that pulse drawing us out toward the edge

I've lived too long too near the edge
stood too close to where it happens
seen what I should not have seen
and heard it all and hear it still
in living dreams I cannot escape

there are people living on the edge
it is true, I have seen them there
clinging to the thin line between them
and the other side of their reality
have stood behind them as they clung
hopeless noses pressed to some window
to some place they could not enter
and I have stayed in the shadows
knowing they would not see me there

I have seen
I have seen
I have seen the best minds of my generation
and they are the same as those seen long ago
and they are not just America
and they are not destroyed after all
nor drag themselves through black streets
but stand waiting arm in arm to hold firm
against that rough beast, its hour come round a
s it slouches unrelenting through every street
seeking some holy land and preordained birth

don't get me wrong and don't get it twisted
many people strive for high ideals
and everywhere life is full of heroism
but what does it matter in the end
what does it matter who is hero and who not
when it may after all be only a dream
and there was nothing at all to see but the rain
through which we come and go like phantoms
as the rain falls like knives slicing the dark
impulse of winter midnight streetlight rain
creating worlds that wash away in a flash
of lightning that wakes us with a start

there are people
cries in the wilderness
there are people
cries in the wilderness
there are people gathered in the streets

flooding the streets of every town and city
cries in the wilderness of grey streets
gathered with pens and with pitchforks
crying for justice all over this land
men and women standing arm in arm everywhere
warning of danger, crying out a warning
cries in the wilderness

in the room the people come and go
talking of what they have seen out there
but they don't go out there and they
and they don't do anything to stop it
in the dark in the room the people watch
in the silence in the room they listen
and drown awash in flickering images
and drown in the battle's sound and fury
across the universe and back again
and still falls the rain like helpless tears

he stands in the shadows of the evening rain
the gentle rain that falls for years
just a little boy standing in the rain
and rain keeps falling like helpless tears
still falls the rain with a sound like the pulse
the pulse of the heart that is changed to the hammer-beat
and rain keeps falling like helpless tears
the boy disappears

still I feel the heartbeat beating underneath every thing
the pulse of the heart that is changed to the hammer-beat
the pulse of the heart that hammers out love
the pulse of the heart that hammers out danger
the pulse of the heart that hammers out a warning
the pulse of the heart that hammers out hatred
while the rain keeps falling like helpless tears
while the best among us lose all conviction
while the worst grow full of passionate intensity
and the heartbeat pulses between every thing

don't get me wrong and don't get it twisted
it may after all have been only a dream
it may be I have seen nothing at all
and there was nothing at all to see in the rain
nothing but a magic shadow-show played in a box
lit by sun and moon against silhouettes of rain
around which we phantom figures come and go
the rain falling like knives slicing the dark
to create worlds then wash them away in a flash
lit by lightning that wakes me with a start

I've lived too long too near the edge
stood too close to where it happens
seen what I should not have seen
and heard it all and hear it still
in living dreams I cannot escape

the words of the prophets echo down the centuries
truth grown tired and worn until the words are only dust
choking off the little breath we gasp to survive
the uncertain future we have created for ourselves
and in the words we hear echoing somewhere distant
the pulsing of a heartbeat pounding like a hammer
and feel that pulse drawing us out toward the edge

surely some revelation is at hand
cries in the wilderness between the lines
this is the way the world ends
cries in the wilderness between the lines
this is the way the world ends
cries in the wilderness between the lines
this is the way the world ends
as we stand waiting arm in arm to hold firm
against that rough beast, its hour come round
as it slouches unrelenting through every street
seeking some holy land and preordained birth
and some ancient anarchy is loosed upon the world

but don't distress yourself with dark imaginings
no doubt the universe is unfolding as it should
and the dark you see is only rain falling
too long living not on the edge like some
too long living in the gutter flows
between the edges where the shadows flow
between the edges able to see the dark
see the dark that consumes their lives

I'm with you in Rockland he shouts out loud
cries from the wilderness with conviction
is anybody out there does anybody hear him
is Rockland just another dream in the dark
his voice an echo of something that is no more
a cry in the wilderness between the lines
I'm with you in Rockland fades in the distance
his voice disappears

but don't get me wrong and don't get it twisted
it may after all have been only a dream
it may be that I have seen nothing at all
and there was nothing at all to see in the rain
and I have disappeared

among the hoodoos: an old house

I.

sunlight flicks across
the hoodoos behind me

there is a feeling here
a power older than time
under a blue bowl of sky t
hat goes on forever

here is no past
       no present
       no future

A man on his own can feel
as the gods must feel

I am Prometheus rising
over one edge of earth
as the sun's light climbs
to meet me at the other edge

I stand at the edge of eternity
of knee level wild grass
facing the sun rising
from the primeval plain

II.

I walk toward the ancient empty house
feel good here above the hoodoos
above the scrub and cacti
above all I've known worlds away

the house has stood a long time empty
paint gone with the prairie winds
most of the glass gone or cracked

the front door lolls open
seems to welcome me

III.

I walk the distance slowly
enjoy the silence of dawn
the soft touch of the morning breeze

I climb the broken steps
cross the verandah
pause before going in

I ease the old door open
the top hinge broken
the bottom one creaking
pull outward
let the outside corner rest
on the verandah's wood floor

I step inside the entrance hall
the door at the end is closed

I pass the archway to the living room
the staircase leading upward
two doorways opposed
on the left and right sides
and open the door to the kitchen

the coal stove is still here
dust covered and spider webbed
traces of rust on the black
on the nickel trim

in another corner
a wooden table and one chair
its back broken

tattered curtains flank broken windows

the whole house is like that
traces of past life

chesterfields and mattresses ripped open
perhaps by mice making nests
by hunters turned vandal from boredom
in each room a piece or two of furniture
never a full complement

IV.

I pause in each room in turn
imagine the life this house has seen
imagine the owners as they were long ago

in my mind I repair the furniture I see
fill the rooms with what is missing
live for a few moments in each room

V.

walking downstairs from the bedrooms
I feel the ancient bannister break away

A Beginning and an Ending

Three knocks of the brass lion
and the door hosts open;
battered conversations
heaved out the doorway
fall flat on silent stairs
and die.
      "Hi. Sorry we're late."
      "He slept until eight."
Tall,
almost handsome;
cute,
rather winsome:
a matched team
joins the celebration.
      "Nonsense!"
      "Hey! Look who's here!"
      "Glad you made it, dear."
      "It's Frank and Sybil!"
Manemass turn eyeballing:
crouching lion silence,
then roar the crowd once more.
gates clang shut
caging the roaring
conversation colosseum
thumbs down crowd.
(Cry blood.)
Enter the gladiators,
in one hand the net
the hazy smoke,
in one hand the whip
wordlash vicious.
Stiletto the room.

Rain

I

Walking out in the rain one day,
met a friend of mine
And we walked our road together a way
And said we both felt fine.

Well the time came that we must part,
My dear, dear friend and I –
As gifts, I gave friendship and she her heart
Baked in an old -style pie.

II

Who are you dreaming of...?
Is it a small child far away
Crying for her mother?
Is it an old woman of another day
Crying for your love?

(It screams with all the latent fury
of the hatred that lies
in love.)

III

Carelessly I ate the humble heart pie –
Digested, divested
Part of a friend; part of a lie;
Part love proved and tested.

IV

Who are you dreaming of...?
Are you dreaming a brand-new life,
The kind you wish you had?
And how real is your dream, or life
Crying out for love?

(It screams with all the latent fury
of the hatred that lies
in love.)

V

Walking out in the rain one day,
met a friend of mine
And we walked along together a way
And said we both felt fine.

VI

The problem is my thoughts are all locked up inside
Peering from a private little cage where they hide...
(Sanity is a strange thing.
You lose it so easily
when you're tired
when you're drunk
when you're angry
when you've lost
a friend
an enemy
a lover
hope.)

VII

A mind is a large empty room
In which two persons meet.

VIII

Who are you dreaming of...?
Is it a small child far away?
Is it an old woman of another day?
Are you dreaming a brand-new life,
And how real is your dream, or life
When there is no love?

(It screams with all the latent fury
of the hatred that lies
in love.)

IX

Walking out in the rain one day,
My dear, dear friend and I –
Part of a friend and part a lie
That said we both felt fine.

X

Who are you dreaming of...
Crying for her mother,
Crying for your love,
The kind you wish you had;
Crying out for love?

(Part a friend and part of me,
it screams with all the latent fury
of hatred that lies.)

Kaleidoscope

My occult fingers twirl the cylinder
And hurried hues whirl past me until
My mind shrinks and I sit very nil
In the great kaleidoscope's centre
Sky purple yellow night rainbower
growing jade raspberry stone-grey still
Flaming shades frame an audible will
Deep in an outdated strobe flower
Fill the air with a maugreered free
Sound oil slick guitar bellowing cow
Now harmonious obscenity
Kodak raindrop feathers shower now
Brilliant bright splendour splashed pure movie
Free flowing kaleidoscope of our now.

The Rose and the Secret Balloon

The red balloon rose
smiling through blue confetti
the man neared
the forked path
his walking stick
swinging
toward the garden.

The purple world hung
on each swing
the stick made
closer to the flowers
and the red
the secret balloon.

Wreak a new horror
retch like an earthworm
earth
as he penetrates
your bowels
and eats
the rose.

The stick enters
the open rose
the burst balloon
blooms and dies
as an afterthought
the man walks on.

The maroon world hangs
on each crimson swing
of the stick
of the flowers
and the red
the secret balloon.

Poet Profile

Bob MacKenzie has been greatly influenced by growing up in Alberta and now finds inspiration for writing during daily walks through woods and along waterfronts in and around Kingston, Ontario. His keen eye for detail shows in his talent for outdoor photography. Bob's ability to draw a wide variety of people into conversation results in astute observations on human nature, and his love of music from diverse genres allows his poetry to sing and dance its way through our complex world.

Bob MacKenzie's poetry has been published across North America and as far away as Australia and India in publications that include The Literary Review of Canada, The Dalhousie Review, Windsor Review, and Ball State University Forum. He's published sixteen volumes of poetry and prose fiction and his work has been featured in numerous anthologies.

Bob has received a number of awards for his writing including an Ontario Arts Council grant for literature, a Canada Council Grant for performance, and a Fellowship to attend the 2017 Summer Literary Seminars in Tbilisi, Georgia.

For eighteen years, Bob's poetry has been spoken and sung live with original music by the ensemble Poem de Terre, and the group has released six albums.

www.ingramcontent.com/pod-product-compliance
Lightning Source LLC
Chambersburg PA
CBHW051235030726
47595CB00003B/915